THIS **SWEET PICKLES** ® BOOK BELONGS TO

_____

In the world of *Sweet Pickles,* each animal gets into a pickle because of an all too human personality trait.

This book is about Goof-off Goose. She'll do everything—tomorrow!

Other Books in the Sweet Pickles Series

Library of Congress Cataloging in Publication Data

Reinach, Jacquelyn.
  Goose goofs off.

  (Sweet Pickles series)
  SUMMARY: Goose continues to put things off in order
to take it easy.
  [1. Geese–Fiction] I. Hefter, Richard. II. Title.
III. Series.
PZ7.R2747Go   [E]   76-44313
ISBN 0-03-018086-4

SWEET PICKLES is the registered trademark of
Perle/Reinach/Hefter.

Printed in the United States of America

Weekly Reader Books' Edition

Weekly Reader Books presents

GOOSE
GOOFS OFF

Written by Jacquelyn Reinach
Illustrated by Richard Hefter
Edited by Ruth Lerner Perle

Holt, Rinehart and Winston · New York

One morning, everybody in the neighborhood was busy
...except for Goose, who was still sound asleep.

Elephant was hanging the wash.
Camel was banging on the roof.
Lion was typing a letter.
Zebra was painting stripes on his house.
Rabbit was hopping about in his garden.

The busy noises woke Goose. She went to the window. "Can't a person sleep in peace?" she honked. "All this hanging and banging and typing and striping and hopping is stopping my beautiful dream!"

Goose closed the window, jumped back into bed and pulled the covers over her head.

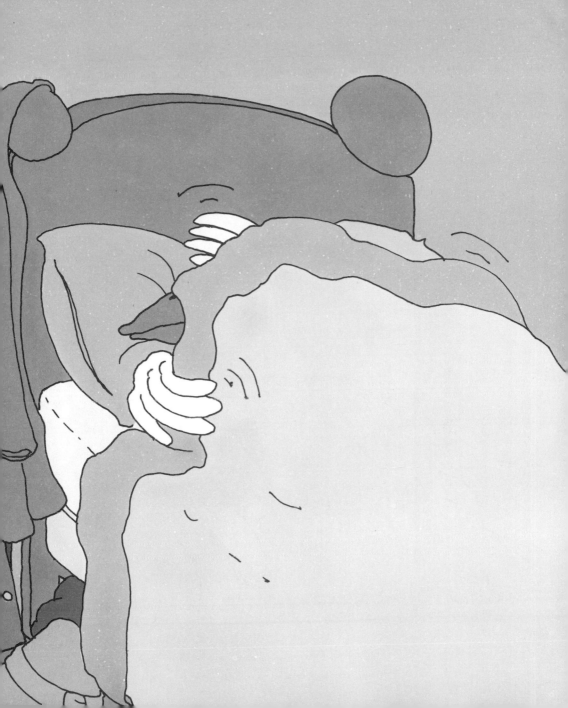

Then a loud blast of music shook the room.

Goose went to the window again. The music was coming from Rabbit's garden. "Your seeding and weeding and hoeing and mowing is bad enough," shouted Goose. "What's going on now?"

"My flowers are listening to music," said Rabbit. "They grow thirty-three and one-third percent faster when they listen to music.

"Would you like to borrow a record for your apple tree?" asked Rabbit. "It could certainly use it!"

ROSES	LOUD MUSIC	4 MINUTES
TULIPS	SOFT MUSIC	9 MINUTES
DAFFODILS	SLOW MUSIC	6 MINUTES
LILACS	FAST MUSIC	1 MINUTE

"Not today," said Goose. "I'm taking it easy today. I'll do it tomorrow."

Goose closed the window, put on her earmuffs, jumped back into bed and pulled the covers over her head.

Then the telephone rang. It was Elephant. "Yesterday you promised that today you'd help me hang the wash," she said.

"I'm awfully sorry," said Goose, "but I'm taking it easy today. I'll do it tomorrow."

"That's what you said yesterday!" snorted Elephant.
"Goodbye!"

Goose put a pillow over the telephone and went back to bed.
But now she couldn't sleep.

"Maybe I'll watch TV," she sighed. She turned on the television set. But there was no picture. "I forgot, the TV's broken," grumbled Goose. "I'll have to get it fixed. But not today. I'm taking it easy today. I'll do it tomorrow."

"Well," thought Goose, "as long as I'm up, maybe I'll have some breakfast." And she went downstairs.

The kitchen floor was all gooey and slippery and wet.

"It seems I forgot to put the ice cream back in the freezer last night," said Goose. "I guess I'll have to mop the floor. But not today. I'm taking it easy today. I'll do it tomorrow."

Just then the doorbell rang. It was Stork bringing in the mail.

He took one step in and slipped.

"Whoops!" he shouted. "I've delivered bowls to moles in deep dark holes and never slipped or tripped! I even delivered a pail of mail to a whale and I didn't get wet! But I've *never* been in a mess like this!"

"Come back tomorrow," said Goose. "The floor will be clean."

"Yesterday you said your mailbox would be clean," said Stork in a huff. "*Good* day!"

"It *is* a good day," thought Goose. "I think I'll take a nap in my hammock."

Goose rolled to one side. Then the other. She tossed. She turned. She counted to ten backwards. She counted to ten forwards. But she couldn't fall asleep. Something felt strange.

It was too quiet!

Goose looked up and down the street. It was empty. "Where is everybody?" she wondered. Then she smelled something delicious coming from Rabbit's house.

She followed the smell.

"Good afternoon, Goose," said Rabbit. "We're having cookies. I baked eleven different kinds. Would you like some?"

"Sure!" said Goose. "But why didn't you invite me?"

"You said you were taking it easy today," answered Rabbit.
"I was," smiled Goose, munching happily. "But that's okay.
I can take it easy tomorrow!"

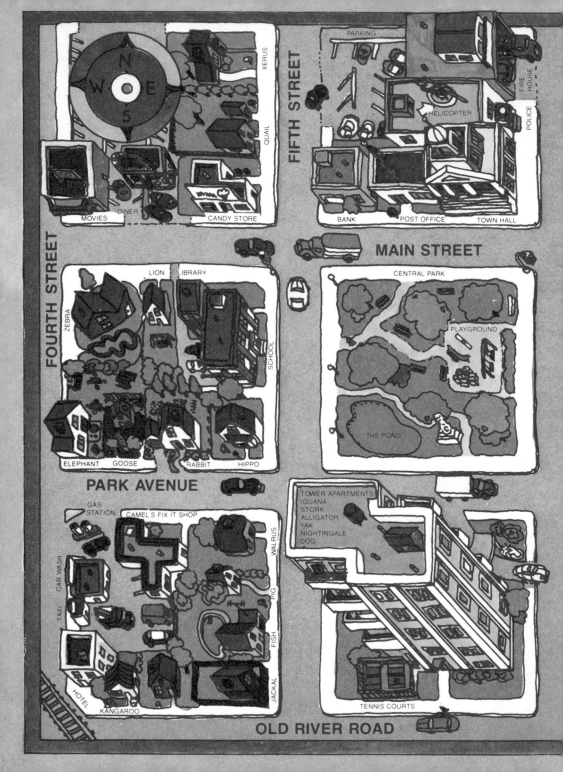